A GIRL'S GUIDE TO CHAOS

by Cynthia Heimel

SAMUEL FRENCH, INC.
45 WEST 25TH STREET   NEW YORK 10010
7623 SUNSET BOULEVARD   HOLLYWOOD 90046
LONDON   *TORONTO*

IMPORTANT BILLING AND CREDIT REQUIREMENTS

All producers of A GIRL'S GUIDE TO CHAOS *must* give credit to the Author of the Play in all programs distributed in connection with performances of the Play and in all instances in which the title of the Play appears for purposes of advertising, publicizing or otherwise exploiting the Play and/or a production. The name of the Author *must* also appear on a separate line, on which no other name appears, immediately following the title, and *must* appear in size of type not less than fifty percent the size of the title type.

A Girl's Guide to Chaos was presented by the American Place Theatre from November 1986 to May 1987. The production was directed by Wynn Handman, with set design by Brian Martin, lighting design by Brian MacDevitt, and costume design by Deborah Shaw; Rebecca Green was production stage manager. The cast was as follows:

CYNTHIA............................Debra Jo Rupp
CLEO .... Mary Portser
RITA...................................... Rita Jenrette
LURENE......................... Celeste Mancinelli
JAKE...................................Peter Neptune*

(In the earliest version of the play, the old man at the end was played by F.D. Herrick.)

---

* Actually Jake was originated by Eric Booth, but he wasn't around very long.

Author's Note: The reader will find the most rudimentary of stage directions, since I simply gave pages of dialogue to the Director, who then staged everything during rehearsal.

But picture this: a simple stage set, with three basic areas, one with a chaise lounge and telephone for Cynthia, another with a table for Cleo, a third with a stool for Rita. Since the furnishings were simple and generic, the actors could quickly move them around to suggest several venues—a restaurant, a terrace, a thrift shop, whatever.

I've updated the play in 1990-91 for the Los Angeles production; specific geographical references pertain to LA instead of New York.

Out on the street, before the play opens, Lurene stands in full clown outfit passing out these flyers to theatergoers:

PPPPPPPPPPPPPPPPPPPPPPP

TOPLESS
HEALTH CLUB

FREE WEIGHTS!
AEROBICS!
SEXY ROSA'S DANCING
SEX KITTENS!

Bottomless Coffee
Free Hot Meatballs
Ask for Rosa!

Pool! Sauna! Massage!

Personality

Reconstruction!

(ask for Rosa)

BRAND NAME
CREDIT CARDS ACCEPTED!
FREE HOT MEATBALLS!
(see Rosa)

UNLUCKY IN LOVE?
MADAME ROSA WILL
FIX EVERYTHING!

left palm – $25–
right palm – ask for details

TAROT!
CRYSTAL BALL!
MEATBALLS!

Rosa's favorite show:

 A GIRL'S GUIDE TO CHAOS – AMERICAN PLACE THEATRE

ddddddddddddddddddddddd

Scene 1: PROLOGUE

CYNTHIA. These are the times that try a girl's soul. We don't know where to turn, what to think. We lie in bed in the morning, desperately searching for a reason to get up. We often wonder if we're in the mood for a sandwich or not.

CLEO. Should we take vitamins? Wear miniskirts? Wax our legs? Demonstrate for animal rights?

RITA. Dance until dawn? Eat natural foods? Search for rich husbands?

CLEO. Take a course in French?

RITA. Become diamond smugglers?

CYNTHIA. Questions cavort in our heads. Crossroads are everywhere. We don't know who we are anymore. Not the way we used to. In the Twenties, we were flappers. We did the Charleston and smoked furtive cigarettes and bobbed our hair. We had plenty of suitors, all who wore center parts and drank gin.

CLEO. In the thirties we were cheerful in the face of adversity, trying not to mind that when the stock market crashed, Daddy lost the mansion and jumped out the window. We became typists and thought ourselves lucky.

RITA. In the forties we were willowy and brave, wearing shoulder pads while we kissed our uniformed men goodbye. Every day we went to factories and filled bullets with gunpowder, every night we sent tender love letters overseas.

CYNTHIA. In the fifties we were pert young housewives sending our gray-flannel-suited husbands to the rat race every morning with square breakfasts in their bellies. We kept up with the Joneses, wore snazzy cocktail dresses and entertained Hubby's boss on our Japanese-lantern-strung patios.

CLEO. In the sixties we let our hair grow wild and fell in love with rock musicians and smoked grass and didn't mind our boyfriends sleeping with everyone in sight, because we were cool. We took the pill or breastfed our babies and tied silly tie-dyed bands around our heads.

RITA. In the seventies, we sought to find ourselves. We hated men and decided to live alone and have a fabulously fulfilling career. We joined consciousness-raising groups and became feminists. We decided not to have children and to find our own space. No one could light our cigarettes without getting a karate chop to the neck.

CLEO. In the eighties we reeled in horror as people kept shoving books at us like "Men who hate women and the women who love them" and magazines told us we have more chance of getting killed by terrorists than getting married. We tried to remember feminism. We learned how to sashay into the drugstore and ask the man for condoms, and we pushed the snooze alarms on our biological clocks.

CYNTHIA. But now what? Whither us? We no longer have role models or prescribed modes of behavior. Things have gone all weird in the world. They're trying to take Roe versus Wade back. The human condition is now being called codependency. Babies have become the new fab party accessory. People who should know better are talking about the child inside themselves. Having sex can kill you. Nobody can get a decent job, a good haircut, or a sane boyfriend.

CLEO. We thought we had them there, back in 1971. "We are women!" we screamed. "You can't fuck us over anymore! We don't *feel* like picking up your socks! We are *bored to death* listening to football stats! We only *pretended* we liked to go fishing! We don't *want* to smile inanely anymore! Ditto washing the floors and diapering! Ditto getting laid when we don't want to! Ditto batting our eyelashes!"

RITA. Pretty good stuff, we thought to ourselves. That ought to stop the bastards in their tracks. And it did. Men are not stupid, or at least not too stupid to realize that if they didn't get sensitive *real fast,* they weren't going to get laid anymore. After all we had put it rather neatly: No equal pay, no pussy.

CYNTHIA. Men really got kind of cute. *"Mea culpa,"* they said to us as they mopped the kitchen floor and basted the pork chops. "We know we did wrong, but we didn't mean it. We know better

now. We'll give you your space. We know where
you're coming from."

CLEO. But things, as they will, went sour.
Men, used to quite a few years of power, found
out that they weren't all that crazy about being
sensitive. Oh, it was a lark for a while, but all that
washing up! All that giving up of jobs! All that
foreplay!

CYNTHIA. What started as a barely
discernible rumble became a deafening roar.

ALL. Fuck it!

CYNTHIA. Men cried in unison all over the
world. "We're not going to take this shit
anymore!"

RITA. It was a devastating blow. One moment
guys were running around not opening doors for
us, the next minute they were either gay, psycho
or gone.

CYNTHIA. The great boyfriend crunch had
begun.

Scene 2: BOYFRIEND CRUNCH

CYNTHIA. 11 a.m. Wake up. Realize I don't
have a boyfriend. Go back to sleep. 12:30 p.m.
Wake up, realize I don't have a boyfriend but am
on the verge of starvation. Stagger into kitchen.
Make coffee. Run mind over assorted boyfriend
possibilities.

1 p.m. Cleo calling from lab. She went to party last night, met cute guy. twenty-four years old, too young. Also has girl friend, but may be breaking up with her soon. He says. We discuss starting a newsletter announcing up-to-the-second status of all heterosexual relationships in L.A. Girls, we figure, would line up outside office on night of publication. We would clean up. Then decide forget it—too much legwork, too depressing. But we digress. Back to cute guy last night. We decide she should call him. Then decide she shouldn't call him, fuck him, who needs him, he has a girl friend. Then decide she should wait a few days. Then call. Maybe. I discuss being lonely. She discusses being lonelier. We decide we're hopelessly neurotic. Women who love too much.

CLEO. Love is funny. Ha ha. I remember love. He smelled like a combination of really fresh tiny lima beans and cotton candy. He wore only shirts with no collars. Eyes like poached eggs. It's over now. There was a question of commitment. Don't we all love that commitment question? What did Dr. Spock tell our mothers to do in 1950? Why are all people in their thirties mentally retarded? Come close, go away, no, come back, fuck you, get outta here I need my space! I love you, oh you love me too? Well, I don't love you after all. It's a crazy endless mating dance with no mating.

RITA. I want a real man. Tall, broad handsome, well-fixed and horny. Do you know what it feels like to have a man say to you "I want you to take your clothes off right now and fuck my brains out" and really mean it? It feels like becoming the first female major league pitcher. It feels like singing a duet with Aretha Franklin. Do you know how long it's been since someone made a pass at me? Maybe two years. Sure, I have dates. Attractive, although skittish dates who are entertaining and charming and invariably fade into a Toyota at the end of an evening. I thought maybe I was just putting out weird vibes, you know, intimidating these sweet and precious little Los Angeles heterosexuals. But everywhere I go I hear the same story from girls, the gist of which is "who do you have to know to get laid around here?" It's chronic, it's epidemic, it's almost passe. After all, we've all been smacked in the face by the 80s, everybody's concerned with status and money and being on the top of the heap. There is mass performance anxiety running amuck in the brains of men. They think they have to be the best. They think they have to write *War and Peace* with their dicks.

CYNTHIA. 2:13 p.m. Call Rita. Complain about being lonely, depressed, sex-starved. Rita interrupts to tell amusing anecdote about self-involved guy who sent her crotchless panties—by messenger. She hates him, thinks he's a wimp pervert. Then she wonders if she has fear of intimacy. Then I wonder if I have fear of intimacy. Decide we both do. Decide to step up therapy so we can have boyfriends.

2:58 p.m. Hang up. Shower. Dress. Go out for breakfast. At corner restaurant see cute guy and give him come hither glance. He pays no attention, is reading *Eat to Win*.

3:20 p.m. Home. Call Chris. She says husband of ten years is having affair, she can tell. Evidence? He disappears every afternoon, then comes home and takes shower. What's wrong with her? she wonders. Decides she has "fear of success" relationship-wise. I remind her of the ten years.

CLEO: We're friends now. Me and him. Except I was over at his house the other day and saw this note. "You were so good last night. Love ya-Kelli." Kelli. Kelli. Kelli. She spells it with an "i" at the end. And she dots the "i" with a circle. I can't stand it. Why are they always named Kelli? Like in *The Heartbreak Kid*? You know that movie where the guy falls in love on his honeymoon? With a blonde bitch named Kelly? They're always named Kelly and they always have straight blonde hair and blue eyes and nothing disfiguring at all about them.

So I had cardiac arrest. "Muriel! Phyllis!" I screamed. "If you have to have a new girl couldn't she have a normal name? Kelli with a goddamned "i" and a circle over the goddamned "i"! "Better a circle over the "i" than circles under the eyes," Mr. Personality said.

RITA. Plus there's feminism. Feminism, our fondest dream. The shock waves are still crashing against our libidos. Men hate treating us as equals, they want to be predators. Strong women are threatening to the fragile male psyche. Men not putting out is simply a fancy version of holding their breath and turning blue. I want to be the object of their desires and the subject of my own life. A difficult feat in 1990, but not impossible. I'll do it or die trying.

CYNTHIA. 4:10 p.m. Call Cleo. She's excited. Cute guy called. Has date tonight.

4:30 p.m. Call from Travis, cowboy in Texas. I think I love him, then wonder if I love him because he's fifteen hundred miles away. Decide I'm a sicko.

5:45 p.m. Feeling peckish. Go to grocery store. Notice two cute guys. Follow one to frozen foods, where other cute guy is waiting. "Shall we have lima beans tonight?" first guy asks second guy. Second guy bursts into tears. "You know I hate limas beans," he sobs.

6:04 p.m. Home. Three messages on machine. Mother, Rita, Chris. Call mother back. She's sad, doesn't have boyfriend. "All the men like younger women," she says, "you must have a million guys." I laugh mirthlessly.

6:52 p.m. Call Chris. Husband having affair, he admits all.

7:45 p.m. Hang up. Read magazine article "How to Spot a Heartbreaker." Take notes.

8:15 p.m. Call Rita back. She'll come over. We'll go dancing.

9:23 p.m. Cleo calls. Date over already. Seems guy suddenly had massive anxiety attack, complete with vomiting and hyperventilating, then admitted he was getting married next week. And ran away. Cleo wonders if I have any Valium. I'm all out.

CLEO. You love somebody and then you don't love them anymore. But if you really love somebody you always love them, don't you? Isn't there always some still small part of you that reads their horoscope in the paper every day?

CYNTHIA. 9:50 p.m. Chris arrives, weeping copiously.

10:02 p.m. Chris's husband arrives, sobbing.

10:10 p.m. Rita arrives. We retreat to bathroom while Chris and husband fight. Terrific sound of breaking glass. We cower and smoke joint.

10:58 p.m. Chris and husband leave after deciding to move to Oregon. Rita and I sweep up.

11:15 p.m. Rita and I go to nightclub. We watch drag queen on stage, singing about how she doesn't have a boyfriend. Rita waves her beer. "Join the club," she shrieks.

2:10 a.m. Drunk, can't find Rita. Cute guy comes up. Looks deep into my eyes. Offers to buy me drink.

3:30 a.m. Cute guy's girl friend comes up, throws drink over his head. Rita appears and restrains her.

4:00 a.m. Home. Realize I still don't have boyfriend. Go to sleep.

Scene 3:   BUSY BEE SCENE

MAN. Day in, day out, sometimes even hourly, I hear pointed references to the fact that there are no available men in this city, that hundreds of thousands of intelligent, attractive, witty, warm and sensitive women are simply withering on the vine, parched for, yet deprived of, crucial and edifying male companionship. According to my statistics, they're dying for it. Here's my question: where are they? I've looked everywhere. I'm desperate for a girl friend. I split up with my last girl a year ago and I still roll over in the middle of the night grabbing for someone who's not there. But I never meet any women. And neither do my friends. Many a night me and my buddies prowl around bars and discos looking for love. Nobody is there. Have all unattached women left town? Do they all have night jobs? Joined convents? What?

CYNTHIA. We're everywhere. Every part of L.A. is riddled with us.

RITA. There we are now, lining up at the cash register at Mrs. Gooch's, clutching a variety of nasty products—calcium so we don't get osteoporosis when we're even older, iron supplements since we suspect we're anemic, oat bran in the vain hope that fiber will help, acidophilus to keep the dread yeast from our door.

CYNTHIA. Amble down Melrose and you'll find several of us eating burgers and fries at

Johnny Rockets, annoyed with ourselves for not being the spinach salad type.

CLEO. Hang a left and five minutes later you'll find a gaggle of us in Betsy Johnson's, trying on a sweater in an ironic attempt to look like Madonna. Keep going and you'll stumble on a few of us at Ecru, wondering how to find the sleeve on an incomprehensively cut cocktail dress. A quick jog up west finds us at Maxfield's, slavering over shoes that cost as much as an Isuzu.

RITA. We're at the dry cleaner imploring them to get the acid-green stain out of the only dress that makes us look willowy.

CLEO. We're at the post office picking up a parcel which we hope will be a surprise tiara, but turns out to be stale cookies from Aunt Selma.

CYNTHIA. We're standing transfixed in the supermarket, staring at the flowers.

RITA. We're fidgeting in bank lines, waiting to use pay phones, collapsing on stairmasters.

CYNTHIA. We're at literary parties, smiling inanely while trying to dredge up something charming to say to the cute man in the green shoes. We're at Book Soup, buying Anne Tyler novels.

CLEO. We're drinking cappuccino everywhere

CYNTHIA. Just walk up to us and say, "Hi there cutie!" Go ahead. See what happens.

JAKE. Hi there, cutie!

CLEO. Well, hi! How are you? Lovely to see you again, gotta rush, goodbye!

JAKE. But you don't know me!

CLEO. I don't? Oh, okay. But then why are you saying hello to me?

JAKE. I think you're cute.

CLEO. Is this scientology? Because thank you for asking, but I've already had my personality tested. Or do you want to sell me a health club membership?

JAKE. Nothing like that. What's your name?

CLEO. Oh, dear. Look, I'm sure you're very deserving but I don't want to sign any petitions or give you bus fare home or try some new hairdressing salon or buy any crack. Thanks anyway, goodbye.

JAKE. Hi there, cutie.

RITA. What did you say?

JAKE. I said, "Hi there, cutie!"

RITA. Is this some new masculine form of patronizing? Do I look so lonely and desperate that I'll talk to any joker on the street who says "Hi there cutie?" Is this some kind of power play?

JAKE. Jesus! I only wanted to say hello!

RITA. Oh, great. Now we're getting abusive. I'll tell you what I don't need in my life, and that's a condescending, abusive man who thinks he can go around calling grown women "cutie." Tell your story walking mister, before I call a cop.

JAKE. Hi there, cutie!

CYNTHIA. Who, me? Why, hello.

JAKE. Great day, right? But then, when isn't it?

CYNTHIA. You look familiar.

JAKE. Oh yeah? Now, if we were in North Dakota, we'd be wearing snow shoes. But here it's perfect. What's your name?

CYNTHIA. Actually, I'm a little chilly. Your face definitely rings a bell.

JAKE. It would be a good day to take a drive to the desert, look for lizards. I've got an old pick-up truck. Nothing fancy, but ...

CYNTHIA. Wait a minute. The Formosa Cafe! Spring, 1988. You were wearing the same green turtleneck. We dated! Twice! We slept together! You never called me again!

JAKE. My god! How are you doing? You're looking great! Jeez, I was a fool! Let's go have coffee.

CYNTHIA. No thank you, I couldn't possibly. My boyfriend would be jealous. And he is the cutest, sweetest guy in the world. The Kiwi!

Scene 4:   INTROS

CYNTHIA. (*To audience.*) The Kiwi. I keep looking at him, at the elegant curve of his jaw, the luxurious curling of his black lashes framing sea-foam eyes, the sensuous yet chiseled mouth, the perfect teeth, the flawless cheekbones, the long, lean body ... My first thought upon seeing him on my doorstep—he was there to paint the kitchen—was "fuck off, you arrogant asshole, you're probably gay anyway, and even if you're not gay, you must be conceited and spoiled, being so stunning."

I am living with a sex object! People treat me differently with my delicious bauble of a man hanging from my arm. Headwaiters snap to attention. The dry-cleaner remembers me. Acquaintances have a new, wary gleam in their eyes—a gleam that, if it could speak, would say "We respect you more now, but don't begin to think we like you any better." Sometimes they even call him "it," as in "It's very beautiful, how big is its dick?"

CLEO. This is my friend Cynthia. We've been friends for ten years. We met at a feminist conference on role models. There was this girl staring fixedly at my feet. Finally she said, "Where did you get those shoes?" Cynthia's madly in love with this guy from New Zealand— the Kiwi—who's incredibly gorgeous but way too young for any self-respecting girl to take seriously.

CYNTHIA. You'd take him seriously in a minute.

CLEO. As far as I'm concerned, the moment you started seeing him he became a eunuch. Oh, the drama! Every other minute she's on the phone— "he says he has a stomach ache, what do you think that means?" "He's been in the bathroom for twenty minutes. Do you think he's trying to tell me something?" They fight about three times a day. Once he told her if she really loved him she'd lose twenty pounds. She threw his saxophone out the window. Occasionally she thinks she's Anna Karenina.

CYNTHIA. I am Dorothy Parker. Everyone knows that. This is Rita, the maniac Texan in our lives. About every third sentence she utters has meaning. It's not all babble. She's kind of deep, kind of raunchy, kind of cosmic. A sculptor. Very wild. Very weird. Likes to go into the desert and shoot at cactus to relieve her finer feelings.

RITA. Watch yourself sugar. Just because we're on this stage doesn't mean I won't punch your lights out.

CYNTHIA. She's honest, forthright, strong, opinionated, and I've never understood why people call her a bitch. She's not a bitch.

RITA. I'm not a bitch. Sometimes I just get a little overexcited. Comes from having had three husbands. Ex-husbands. And really I never was the mellow type. I figure I'll have plenty of time to be mellow when I'm dead. Don't forget to say I hate radicchio.

CYNTHIA. Rita's idea of a gourmet meal is chicken-fried steak with a side of grits, hold the salad. Her motto is "If you can't fry it or fuck it, forget it."

RITA. I am a woman with my priorities in order. You won't catch me sporting a Chanel handbag. Now have you all met Cleo?

CLEO. You're about to thave the pleasure. I'm a scientist. I'm smart. I'm exceedingly well-dressed. If only I were attractive to men.

RITA. They follow her down the street. They lie prostrate on her doorstep. They pelt her with propositions.

CLEO. When? When did any such thing happen?

CYNTHIA. She's riddled with insecurity, our Cleo. And she suffers from selective blindness. She only notices men who wouldn't have her on a bet. But we do wear the same shoe size.

CLEO. Come on. I can never get dates. You two always have guys. I've *never been married.*

RITA. So?

CLEO. There's something wrong with me.

CYNTHIA. See? A nutburger. But adorable. And works hard. May well discover the cure for cancer in her spare time.

CLEO. I can do differential equations in my head.

RITA. How many of you can say that? And this is a man.

JAKE. Hello.

CYNTHIA. Any man. Sometimes he's my ex-boyfriend Jake who I lived with for three years.

JAKE. Hello.

CLEO. Sometimes he's someone else. Think of him as generic. Isn't he cute?

JAKE. Hi!

RITA. Should we introduce Lurene?

CYNTHIA. Who's Lurene?

CLEO. You know, the one who has a million part-time jobs and we're always running into her? The one who says she actually wouldn't mind cleaning your apartment? The one who was in the clown outfit handing out flyers when we came in here?

RITA. Lurene's a tough cookie. She can introduce herself.

LURENE. Listen, did any of you not get one of these flyers? I mean, if you didn't could you raise your hand now? Because I have to go now. I've got to get to my waitress gig. I'm already late.

Scene 5: THE L.A. NICOLA SCENE

LURENE. I work at L.A. Nicola. A goofy place, full of insane jazz musicians, carpenters-slash-photographers-slash-directors on the make and blotto English people spouting hyperbole. Everybody knows everybody, some people come here for the food, but most of them just like to hear their ideas floating around. Me, I come for the tips.

CYNTHIA. Don't you wish that you could just pull certain people aside and say, "Can we discuss your outfit for a moment? I think you should reconsider."

RITA. Absolutely. The woman is an eyesore. I see her in putty-colored cotton jersey, a smidgen of blusher and her hair back to its natural color.

CLEO. (*Walking in.*) Yo! What's up? Dissecting that turquoise number with the clown makeup? I see her in pale peach linen.

CYNTHIA. Heads up girls, I've got a column to get out.

RITA. Does that mean you've been lying on your chaise all day reading fashion magazines?

CLEO. Looking for material?

CYNTHIA. I want to write about women, how they relate to men.

RITA. I know! You want our help. I won't do it. Why should we discuss our thoughts about men so you can steal our words and concepts, as usual.

CYNTHIA. What are you, a sculptor, going to do with your words? Put them in the lobby of a bank building?

RITA. Maybe.

CLEO. I don't want men to know what I think.

CYNTHIA. Don't be silly. Men and women are no longer enemies. We've reached a new plateau in the womens' movement. We need to *understand* each other, be *generous* with each other.

MAN IN FLAMINGO SHIRT. Excuse me ladies, may my friends and I join you?

CYNTHIA. Get lost, creep. Anyway, if men knew what makes us tick, if they understood our little foibles ...

RITA. Foibles? Excuse me, but foibles? What foibles are these?

CYNTHIA. Okay, maybe not foibles, but you know the things they complain about—we're always late; we can never make up our minds; we never care about baseball standings; we get jealous all the time; we hate for them to go out drinking; all we care about are dresses and children; we refuse to have major political discussions; we hate giving head—you know.

CLEO. Let's not talk about giving head, let's talk about dresses. I love talking about dresses. Write this down. The study of clothes should be up there with the study of nuclear physics, or possibly higher. The placement of a hemline, the tuck in a bodice, the thickness and nap of a fabric—all these things are riddled with meaning so deep and far-reaching that the findings would rock humankind if only someone would pay attention.

RITA. That's what men think about the Superbowl. Only we don't get it. But we can look at a woman in a turquoise dress and figure out where she bought it, why she bought it, what her house looks like, what books she reads, how often she has sex.

CLEO. She got it at Loehmann's. She bought it because she thought the shoulder pads would minimize her hips; she lives in Canoga Park and her kitchen is done in daisy contact paper; she considers *Fear of Flying* a work of art; and she has sex twice a month with someone whose name is either Norman or Josh.

RITA. No way. His name is Eric. I can tell.

CLEO. My point is, clothes are as much a science as Monday night football. But do men bring us popcorn and beer while we shop? No. Okay, now I'm ready to talk about giving head.

CYNTHIA. Let's not talk about giving head. Let's talk about jealousy.

CLEO. Why can't we talk about giving head?

CYNTHIA. Because I'll never forget your sperm-facial fiasco.

RITA. My last boyfriend before Elroy told me our relationship was crippled by an insistent subterranean hum of neurotic jealousy that emanated from my brain. And he was right. I am the jealous type. It started with my little sister, that time I shaved her head and told her she looked like Grace Jones. I knew I was weird.

CLEO. The worst thing about jealousy is that you lose not only the will to live but also your sense of humor. Mel Brooks could come to dinner and a jealous person would only say, "Pass the potatoes."

LURENE. I once hired a private detective to follow my husband around.

OTHERS. Why? How come? Really?

LURENE. Well, he once told me something. Oh, by the way, these drinks are on that fellow over there in the flamingo shirt. The one chatting with that girl in the turquoise dress. Someone should talk to her. Shoulder pads aren't everything. Anyway, once my husband said to me, "Lurene, every man in the world wants to fuck every woman he can, and the only reason he doesn't is that his girl friend or wife would eat him for breakfast." I've never been the same.

CYNTHIA. I think he was right. Men do have an overwhelming lust to conquer.

CLEO. Men have an overwhelming lust to lust. It's built into them biologically. They want to put it everywhere. Let's talk about giving head.

RITA. So we get jealous. Who can blame us? We want to nest, they want to forage.

CYNTHIA. I don't want to nest.

LURENE. Yes you do, hon.

CYNTHIA. I wasn't aware that we'd met.

LURENE. No need to get huffy, doll. I see you in here with your boyfriend, the one who always wants to know exactly which river the trout comes from. Another girl looks at him, you look back daggers. Rightly so, too. He's gorgeous. Whoops! Well, I'd better get back to my other tables. (*Exits.*)

CYNTHIA. I'll break her kneecaps.

MAN. Permit me to interrupt. Being an ex-reporter, I am also an inveterate eavesdropper, and I want to say you're wrong. Men may like to fuck around, but their jealousy, when aroused, is awesome. Actually, women only have one major flaw. They are manipulative and greedy.

RITA. Wha? (*Simultaneously.*) CLEO. Nooo!

MAN. Hear me out. I'm a rich guy. Wrote a magazine piece about a teenaged heroine addict/transvestite which became a movie of the week. I met a few people. So now every woman I go out with expects me to introduce her to

Warren. Half of them angle for a car, the other half want a fur coat. I like to hang out in this dive, but if I don't take them to Spago they whimper. You women demand to be treated as equals, yet at the same time you want to be taken care of. This infuriates me.

CLEO. Well, I'm not like that.

RITA. I don't even know anybody like that.

CLEO. You're the one who's been plying us with drink.

LURENE. Hey Fred! Telephone

MAN. Excuse me, I'll be right back.

CYNTHIA. How rich do you think he is?

CLEO. I wouldn't mind meeting Warren.

RITA. Jesus, do you think he's right?

CYNTHIA. Let's talk about jealousy.

Scene 6: JEALOUSY MONOLOGUE

CYNTHIA. Worst thing in the world happened the other day. I was looking for a book and came across a secret cache of letters. Well, okay, *one* letter. The Kiwi was in England, thousands of miles away, and here was this letter I'd never seen before. Girlish handwriting. What to do? I read the breezy little missive in a flash. Old girl friend pining away for him. Lying in bed, eating salted nuts, drinking hibiscus tea, thinking about him.

Drinking hibiscus tea. Thinking about him. The cow. The slut. The tramp. The tart. The troll.

By 2:30 a.m. it was clear I could never see him again—difficult since he lived with me but not impossible. By 3:30, I realized I had no choice but to seek this woman out and ruin her life. By five, they were both stone cold dead, victims of a brutal bloodbath, and I was appearing at his funeral all in black, with an enigmatic smile behind my tasteful veil.

Ever have a fight transatlantically? Every well-chosen invective costs about $2.75. "If you are not home on the next flight you will not only never see me again but I will melt down your saxophones and dance on your guitars with hobnailed boots." $87.50.

My paranoia was baroque. I had, I figured, simply discovered the tip of the iceberg. Actually, he was making it with every woman I had ever known, or seen. Maybe with men, maybe with dogs. When I tried to make breakfast I threw the toast across the room in a fit of frenzy. I took a Valium. Dissolved into tears. Finally called Cleo at work.

I found this letter.

CLEO. Come right over. (*To audience.*) Here we go, Drama City. Do you think she's overreacting? I think she's overreacting.

CYNTHIA. Overreacting? How about that bit where she can't wait to feel his arms around her again.

CLEO. Again is an extremely imprecise adverb. And remember, *she* wrote the letter, he didn't. She's obviously a silly bimbo and may well be harkening back to years ago. Believe me, this is a letter from a desperate hibiscus tea drinker.

CYNTHIA. She's going to be a lot more desperate after I've shoved a couple of knitting needles in her eyes.

Overreacting?

He was sitting in our living room, gray-skinned and shaking.

"Jesus Christ, she wrote the letter, I didn't. I can't control what she does." Even the bags he had thrown in the doorway looked forlorn and frightened.

He denied everything.

I kept at him.

He kept denying.

At 6 a.m. he was crazed with jet lag and desperate for sleep. "Just tell me the truth," I said. "It will be all right. I won't mind. I just want to know. "Well," he said, I'm really sorry, but we did do it once.

I kicked him in the stomach. "Get out of this house right now, you scumbag! You toad! Don't come back or you're a dead man. There are two, count 'em, morals to this story:

1. Don't leave incriminating letters lying around.

2. Don't look for trouble.

These two morals are intertwined. A person who leaves letters around the house is down on his hands and knees groveling for trouble. Being a firm believer in the there-are-no-accidents school of life, I refuse to believe that my lover left that bombshell around by mistake. I think things were going too smoothly. I think he wanted to stir things up. The passive-aggressive weasel.

And what kind of moronic impulse made me read it? I think things were going too smoothly. I think I wanted to stir things up. I am a masochistic nit.

Here is a rule I have discovered too late. Do not feed paranoia. It is not only good manners to give one's lover his privacy, it is in one's own self-interest. Searching for infidelity is totally self-destructive. And paranoia (read my lips) is nothing but self-punishment.

This is what I keep telling myself. It's not working. He goes out for coffee, takes an extra five minutes, I'm suspicious. He comes home from band practice, takes a bath, I'm suspicious. He goes to work in the morning, I'm suspicious. He says he has a headache at an intimate moment, I want him terminated.

(*Goes to Rita.*) What can I do? I'm driving myself crazy.

RITA. You'll get over it in a couple of months. Sexual jealousy is a deep primeval emotion, contrary to what those nitwits in the sixties used to say—remember how they used to tell us we should and love each other and fuck everybody and not feel the teensiest possessive? We are all deeply protective of our sexual property—it's like a monster that lurks in our depths.

Occasionally the monster surfaces, as when some imbecilic kiwi leaves incriminating letters where paranoiac girls can find them. And when the monster is stirred, it takes a while for him to subside. But he'll go away again, providing there isn't another incident.

CYNTHIA. If there is, the man is dogmeat.

RITA. If there is, he is history. If you don't kill him, I will. Any man who obliquely informs his girl friend regularly that he is fucking around is nothing but a heap of pigshit. Once is horrible. Twice is unforgivable.

CYNTHIA. (*Eager:*) So you think I should forgive him?

RITA. What the hell, give it a shot.

CYNTHIA. You know the worst part, Rita? Not the infidelity, the betrayal. As horrible as it is to envision his body intermingled with another's, while she pants and squeals and he presses his ...

RITA. You're not at all well.

CYNTHIA. As bad as all that is, it is worse knowing he lied to me, kept a secret from me.

RITA. Darlin', that's enough. This man is not just an extension of you. He has his own life, his own problems. Why the hell should he tell you outright? This is life, hon, not the soap opera of your dreams.

CYNTHIA. Oh, yeah?

RITA. Let it go. You gotta trust them, even when you're not sure they're trustworthy. Trust them or leave them. Nothing else will work. Trust me.

Scene 7: JAKE MONOLOGUE

JAKE: Now I was monogamous. Faithful old Jake. Cynthia was more than enough for me to handle. We lived together for three years. I think I scared her away. I came on too strong. I knew what I wanted and I took it. Tried to take it. You know what she used to love? Going to the supermarkets at three in the morning. She was always looking for the plums with the red meat inside them. She'd get this excited look in her eye as she stuck her thumbnail into each plum.

Women! There's someone else I have my eye on now. It's a little complicated. Don't even ask. And you know, I'm trying to do it just right. I don't call every day. I call maybe every fourth day. And I try for nonchalance. (*Whistles, twiddles fingers.*) "So like, wanna go a movie maybe?"

I've gotten nowhere. She doesn't even know I exist. I think. I don't know. I'm confused.

Here's my theory: You live in Los Angeles of all places, in 1990 of all times, and you can't help it, you're totally self-involved.

We all not only think we're the center of the universe and about to become famous in a second, but we're completely self-conscious. Like me being nonchalant. Like me searching my soul for the proper place to take her for cappuccino to make a good impression. Is Rebecca's too yuppy? Is Hugo's too bright? I edit what I say—I remember in the 60s when you could just say "Come here woman!" and then in the 70s you just got a look in your eye like your puppy died and said, "I know I shouldn't be telling you this, but I cry sometimes, late at night." In the eighties you let your beard grow for three days, wore black, and tried to look psychotic but tender. Now I don't know. So I just say what comes into my mind. That doesn't work either. I mean, what's the big deal? Why is searching for a mate suddenly on the scale of the Crusades? Why can't we just be with someone, say, "Okay, I have fun with you, I like to sleep with you, you're the one for me, I'm going to stop looking now."

Hah! Wake me when we get things figured out.

Scene 8:   RITA AND CLEO
PRIVATE CHAT

CLEO. Oh, I don't know, I don't know. What am I going to do? I'm just not the type. I mean, the minute a friend gets involved with man, I no longer see him as available, ever. I would never go out with a girl's boyfriend. It's not done. It deserves the death penalty.

RITA. Okay sugar, which girl's boyfriend are you going to steal?

CLEO. Oh my God oh my God. Cynthia's.

RITA. Now Cleo. Look at me. Listen to what I'm saying very, very carefully. Are you paying attention? Good. Don't do it. Don't even think about doing it. Girl, you do value your face don't you? She'll rip it off your head. Hon, she'll shoot you in the foot. Not only that, but I'll kill you myself.

CLEO. Listen, it's not my idea. He just keeps calling and calling. He stutters when he asks me out. It's so cute.

RITA. And where is Cynthia when he's making all these calls?

CLEO. Home I guess. Playing house with the baby Kiwi.

RITA. Are we in the movie Gaslight?

CLEO. Gaslight? Was that with Joseph Cotton?

RITA. Cleo, you're driving me mental. You said you were going after Cynthia's boyfriend. The Kiwi is her boyfriend.

CLEO. No, no, no, I mean Jake, of course. What do you think I am, suicidal? Her ex-boyfriend. I have a little trouble with the space-time continuum.

RITA. Well, Jesus, Jake. That's a relief. But I see what you mean. It'll still be weird.

CLEO. She'll hate it. She'll just hate it. I'll have nothing more to do with him. What could I have been thinking?

Scene 9:   COUPLES

CYNTHIA. I'm a couple! I never thought I'd enjoy it. But I do. I do. We do couple things. We say "we," as in "we saw this great movie the other night" or "we need a blender!" We are so tedious! I love it! It feels safe and warm and adorable.

JAKE. I only like couples when they're not really couples. I get depressed when I'm around two people who have turned into a single unit. And some of the couples that are running lose on the street these days ... like Fred and Wanda baby talk. (*To Rita.*) Hewwo, widdle diddums, did you miss your qweat big Fweddie bear?

RITA. Oh, Fweddie, me never going tawk to you again! Me afwaid! You come home twenty minutes late!

JAKE. I had a itsy bitsy meeting wiff the head of the corporation, widdle dumpling! We going to nail Dupont Chemical to the wall, my teensy weensy.

RITA. OOOH! Big mean Fweddy!

CLEO. You wanna talk about the couple from hell? How about Geoffrey and Elaine snotfest? Geoffrey darling, pass the organic, unborn baby lettuce. And the wine from the adorable little village near Auswitz.

JAKE: Not Auswitz pet, Dachau. Darling, you know I'm not absolutely sure I *like* white truffle ravioli. Especially with shitake mushrooms. I feel it is too much of a cliche.

CLEO. It's true, truffles are being sadly overused. Do you know what Gloria served us at her "Save the rhinos in rainforests" tea the other day? Oh Geoffrey, you won't believe it, you just won't! Pesto!

JAKE. Priceless! And she calls herself a trendsetter!

CLEO. But we know better, don't we dearest? Frozen ding-dongs for dessert!

JAKE. Angel! So post-modern!

RITA. How about my personal favorites, Bob and Gloria Fistfight? Aren't they a stitch at parties? Oh Bob, I hate you, I hate you! You're disgusting.

JAKE. Gloria, you are so neurotic. You're overreacting, as usual. Isn't she overreacting, everybody? Isn't her Electra complex showing?

RITA. You child! You infant! Do you all know what this man did? You'll never believe it! He burst into tears during an AT&T commercial! Reach out and touch someone! Reach out and touch a shallow, sentimental wimp, I thought. Oh, God, what am I doing with you?

JAKE. So I cry! Plenty of women like a man who cries! I want a divorce!

RITA. So do I!

CLEO. (*Gives Jake a meaningful glance, or meaningful kick.*) Okay guess who this is. Oh motherfucking Christ I have so much to do! Three columns due today. Oh well, maybe I'd better just lie on the couch and read fashion magazines. Maybe I'll get an idea.

JAKE. Cynthia, you're so earthbound. The reason you lie around on the couch all day is because you're malnourished. You should be drinking wheat grass juice every day. Then you'd be peppy.

CLEO. What do you know about life, you baby pipsqueak? You want peppy? Date Luci Arnaz. Go away, I'm thinking.

(*JAKE moves.*)

CLEO. Where do you think you're going?
CYNTHIA. Okay, enough, enough, I get it. You're trying to ruin everything. Isn't it funny how nobody ever likes to see somebody happy? But I'm not going to get upset.

Scene 10:   MYRNA SCENE

You know how sometimes, when you're upset or angry or just plain mentally ill because your lover has just been callous or stupid or totally disgusting? And you know that the minute you open your mouth you're going to turn into your mother? And your mother whined and you don't want to do that so you sit there and fester and grow strange and get cancer?

I have the answer. It's so easy. One night I was sitting around watching *The Thin Man* on TV, and William Powell had just outsmarted

Myrna Loy by putting her into a cab. She thought he was getting in beside her and they were going to catch a murderer, but instead he told the cab to take her to Grant's tomb and the cab sped away, containing an astonished Myrna. When her darling husband later asked her how she liked Grant's tomb, what did Myrna do?

No, she didn't say you are a filthy pig and I'm calling my lawyer, she didn't snivel and whine about how she'd never get over what he'd done to her, she didn't overdose on sleeping pills, she just said, nice as you please "It was lovely. I'm having a copy made for you." Suddenly, I had this enormous epiphany! When in doubt, act like Myrna Loy!

This is the last self-help program you'll ever need—the Myrna Loy way of being. Forget the twelve steps, forget years of grueling psychotherapy!

I sure have. Whenever I'm too crazy, too paranoic, or too mentally feeble to cope with a situation, I pretend I'm Myrna. It's magic.

Consider Myrna in the movies. A real pip. Witty, self-possessed, adventuresome, wore great hats. This is good stuff. Myrna is the perfect role model for these perilous times. Only last summer I avoided a major catastrophe: There I was in England with The Kiwi, minding my own business, when he suddenly decided nothing would do but that we must climb Glastonbury Tor, a small mountain, in the dark, for religious reasons. He was sure we would see God. I was sure I would stumble and break all my bones. He insisted. I wouldn't budge. He went anyway, taking my cigarette lighter as a torch, leaving me alone on some wet rocks.

When the thoughtless cad reappeared, my first impulse was to sniffle. The words that were clamoring to spring from my lips went like this: After all I've done for you, look how you treat me! You obviously don't care about me at all! What have I done to deserve this?

The trouble with the what-have-I-done-to-deserve-this ploy is that people will tell you. and who needs her faults enumerated when she's already in a bad mood?

Some still, small voice of sanity cautioned me that this was the wrong tack, even though it was the one I was brought up with. Like a lightning bolt, Myrna flashed through my sniveling brain.

I held my peace in the car ride home, letting Loyness filter through my being. When we got inside the house, I calmly filled the kettle and turned around.

"Darling," I said. "You are a maggot. A brat. Being abandoned on a dark hillside is not my idea of a good time. Next time the climbing lust overtakes you, leave me home. I will have my hair done."

"But," he tried to say.

"Don't 'but' me, you shit," I continued silkily. "I simply will not have it. And that's that."

Yes, okay, the words were a bit clumsy, since I had to write my own dialogue on the spot. But things never got ugly. By morning, he apologized passionately, I accepted lustily. We were in perfect accord as I slipped into my satin dressing gown to go down for breakfast.

Myrna would have been proud.

Scene 11:   SEX TIPS

RITA. Now I have a code that involves no movie stars. It's so simple and eloquent that you will hit your head in wonderment and say "Now why didn't I think of that?" Here it is:

Never lead a sensible life.The moment you decide that you're a grownup now, and must put away foolish things like dancing all night or cruising down strange highways is the moment you develop crow's feet.

Have adventures, opt for the unknown. Forget fears, fear gets you nowhere. God protects drunks, infants, and feisty girls, girls who are up for anything.

CLEO. Then I'm in for a lot of trouble.

RITA. Shun boredom! We must quit dull jobs, leave tedious men. And we will be fine, since nature abhors a vacuum.

CLEO. That's not strictly true ...

RITA. Cultivate a deviant attitude! Unless we're vigilant, we could turn into zombies. Seed pods are furtively placed in our bedrooms while we sleep, and the next thing we know we're craving feminine hygiene deodorant and Hamburger Helper. This kind of behavior is called, funnily enough, normal. It is not normal, it is depraved and sick to do what other people expect.

CLEO. That's all very well, but what about the *really* deep and far-reaching issues? Like, here's what I want to know—should you ever sleep with a man on the first date?

CYNTHIA. No you should not. No matter that he crushes you at your door in an embrace so flattening that you inadvertently buzz every doorbell in your apartment building. No matter that he falls to his knees and grasps the hem of your skirt, sobbing and pleading and promising rubies. No matter that you've worshipped him afar since he was twelve. No matter that you haven't had an ounce of sex since the spring before last and you're afraid you'll dry up. No matter that he's just won the Nobel peace prize. Even if he promises to halt all nuclear weapons activities, don't do it. This is a hard and fast rule, there are no exceptions.

Except if you really want to.

But make sure you kiss him before you go to bed with him, and pay careful attention. Does he thrust his tongue down your throat as if he's searching for the Holy Grail? Does he smash his teeth against your lips? If so, drop him flat. A man who can't kiss can't fuck.

CLEO. Sometimes you decide you'll probably die if you don't go to bed with him that instant and then when you finally do it, he can't get it up. Does that only happen to me?

CYNTHIA. Yes.

RITA. Ain't it a kick in the head when that happens? But I don't worry much about first night, or even second night jitters. That's just nerves. Pressure. Fear. I swear if I were a man I don't know if I'd ever be able to get it up with a new person. But if we're talking prolonged, chronic impotence, chances are you have a guilty man in your arms.

The most common cause of impotence is marriage to other women. The penis knows its ten commandments, and this is its own, quirky way of slapping its owner's hand.

"Don't touch," the penis says.

"But I want to," pleads the man.

"I don't care," says the penis, "its just not done, old sport. You've got that nice little woman waiting for you at home."

"Just this once, now that I've gotten this far?"

"No. If I let you this time, then you'll want just one more time, and one more time after that and pretty soon we won't know where we are."

"I know where I wish *you* were."

"Well, I'm not going there. It's not right. Now quit this nonsense and let's go home."

CLEO. Jeez. Men are such sensitive flowers.

CYNTHIA. Which is why it's necessary to practice the golden rule when in bed. It's true that there is a certain informality inherent in being naked, and that makes it all the more important to be strict with one's social graces. One must be polite. It is not polite to laugh and point at the penile member.

CLEO. Sometimes you want to, though. Just to liven things up. It is also not polite to break into long spasmodic sobbing. Or say that your last lover did it exactly the same way. Or discuss running sores. Or imitate Joan Rivers. Or start snoring while one's partner's head is between one's legs. Or ask if it's in yet.

RITA. Cleo! You never!

CLEO. Well, I was always only kidding. But I've learned there's a time and a place for jokes.

CYNTHIA. I don't know. I think jokes are always appropriate. But sweet, nice, loving jokes. Cleo, did you really ever ask ...?

CLEO. Okay, so I get testy sometimes. I have to admit it. I like big ones. Not huge or anything. But, you know, good size. Do all your ex-boyfriends have big ones, Cynthia?

CYNTHIA. Why?

CLEO. Nothing.

RITA. What's good size? Six inches? Seven?

CLEO. Eight. Or nine. After nine it gets problematical.

RITA. And after ten it hurts.

CYNTHIA. Well, I don't think it matters at all if you love him.

RITA. Well, darlin, it doesn't exactly *matter*. It's just nice they're big, that's all. Pleasant to look at. Any girl who pretends different is just working overtime on being one of them total women. Or else she's a social worker. But it doesn't exactly *matter*, when you get right down to it. Vernon ...

CLEO. Vernon?

RITA. Vernon, one of my ex-husbands, had this ittybitty cock, and that man still to this very day drives me insane with lust. If he walked in here right now, I'd be on him like a duck on a junebug.

CYNTHIA. Thick ones are always nice.

RITA. I like a thick one myself.

CLEO. Who doesn't?

RITA. This is making me horny.

CYNTHIA. I've been making an informal study of horniness and have discovered that being horny is not always felt at its source, but can instead be manifested by blurry vision, mouth dryness, heart palpitations, numbness in the extremities, nausea, and of course the ever-popular liquidity in the loins. Could this be a column?

RITA. You're not horny. You've got a boyfriend.

CYNTHIA. Definitely a column. The top ten warning signs of horniness. One: You exist. Two: When introduced to a man you immediately wonder what it would be like to shower with him. Three: When driving in a foreign sports car, you find yourself gazing contemplatively at the gearshift.

CLEO. I've been so horny I've thought of putting on a black see-through nightgown, setting a fire in the living room, and calling the fire department.

CYNTHIA. Firemen! Every girl's forbidden dream. Four: Merv Griffen begins to look good to you.

RITA. This is just making me worse.

CLEO. Instead of having breakfast, you masturbate.

RITA. I wish you two would stop.

CYNTHIA. Okay. Sorry (*Giggle.*) we'll stop. You wonder if the twelve-year-old down the street is old enough yet.

RITA. I AM NOT AMUSED!

CYNTHIA. Yes you are. You have to be. What else is there?

CLEO. Here's what I wish. I wish that you could tell, before you got to bed with a man, whether he likes oral sex.

LURENE. They love you to do it to them but do they return the favor?

RITA. I don't want to talk about this.

LURENE. Yes, you do hon. Some men love oral sex and will dive right for it with the slightest encouragement. If you find a man like this, treat him well. Feed him caviar and don't let your girl friends catch a glimpse of him.

But occasionally even the best of men will balk at muff-diving. He will start glancing at his watch and muttering about an urgent appointment. One can understand this sort of man's feelings. And one can despise these feelings. It is every red-blooded girl's duty to put this sort of man straight, pronto. A suggestion ... tell hm you know for a fact that Bruce Springsteen wouldn't be caught dead not giving a girl head.

CLEO. Gaze wistfully into the distance and say "You *are* a pet, Harold, and I *am* devoted to you. But I'm afraid no man can ever satisfy me. Ah, there was a time, very long ago, when I was thrilled and delighted beyond my wildest dreams (here's where you let a wistful smile play across your face). There was a man, you see, who put his head between my legs and well, ah, he *licked*. I was crazy with desire, Harold. I became a veritable animal. Ah but (another wistful smile) I don't suppose I could ever hope to feel so passionate again.

RITA. Know what I did once? I told this guy I read somewhere, I thought it was probably *Forbes*, that the only men who make it to the top economic bracket are those who eat pussy on a regular basis.

CLEO. Did it work?

RITA. I think so.

LURENE. Get into bed upside down.

That's what I do, anyway, my husband's not the subtle type. Come to think of it, neither am I.

I'm too busy trying to make it in this city to think about sex. I mean I think about it. But it's not knotty. Not the big problem. I mean, look at me. I'm busy. You might see me at any health club or picking up a smudgy-faced three year old girl at a day care center. You wouldn't know that my thoughts are running a mile a minute. I'm a thinker. I've got a philosophy of L.A. survival.

Here's my first philosophical point: Never listen to anybody. What do they know? The first thing somebody will tell you in Hollywood is that everything is connections. Meet the right person and you'll make it big. Like last week I was catering this party and there was this big movie star there, you probably know him, Jack somebody. Big guy. Big deal. So this Jack guy is with this girl named Meryl someone and all these people they're all over Jack and Meryl at this party and I could see all these eyes devouring these two movie stars—the greed and yearning was right in my face while I served the cold potato soup—it was like "look this way, Jack and Meryl, make me a big star, notice me!" Jack and Meryl looked like they wanted to throw up in their shoes.

The only way to make it in this city is to work yourself half to death and then work some more. Keep your eye on what you want and stick with it. Because Jack and Meryl don't want to know you until you can tell them something they don't know. Am I right?

Also, this is very important: Everybody's gotta have an angle in this burg. It's what they live for. I let 'em. So I forget to rewind my videotape and I gotta pay a dollar. So the florist overcharges a few cents for a tulip. Am I going to make a big scene and have a cardiac arrest? No thank you, not with the laundry to do. Not when the kid has to play the baby Jesus in the school nativity. I'll let people take a little advantage here and there. I'll keep cool and not worry about who's screwing me, since everybody's screwing everybody and where's the percentage worrying about little tiny screws?

Here's something you have to do: Keep away from the experts. You know, people with overviews. You know the type—the ones who have a total handle on the situation in Iraq or the world's biggest authority ever on psychology. These are the people who have something to hide. Now I'm not saying all these people are morons. I'm just saying *most* of them are morons. Experts with overviews are always the ones who forget that their best friend just had root canal, or their kid has a problem with math, or that it's their sister's birthday.

I notice details. And I bet God does too. I need an overview, I go to the top. I bet God is in the back of the refrigerator, hanging out behind that moldy tuna casserole, noticing whether you give your kid enough milk. God is a fly on the wall at the coffee shop, seeing if you short change the waiter. Angelinos, I swear, can be the kindest people on earth. And God notices tiny kindnesses.

If God exists that is. I'm not sure. I think so.

Scene 12: PHONE CALLS

JAKE. Cleo?

CLEO. Jake?

JAKE. I'm thinking about you all the time.

CLEO. Well, I don't think about you. I wish you'd stop this. We're just good friends, Jake.

JAKE. Well, okay then. I guess I'll be going.

CLEO. Jake!

JAKE. What!

CLEO. I, um. Well. I think about you too. Sometimes.

JAKE. Let's go to a movie tonight. Something.

CLEO. Cynthia's my best friend, Jake.

JAKE. So fucking what! She won't give a goddamn. She's head over heels with that Kiwi infant. We're history. She dumped me three years ago. This is crazy. This isn't friendship, it's tyranny! What kind of complicated code do you women have, anyway?

CLEO. Look maybe you're right. I'll think about it, okay? It goes against the grain, but I'll think about it. But please, don't push me.

JAKE. I know, I know, I'm too pushy. It's my fatal flaw. I should see a shrink.

CLEO. Cut it out, Jake. You're perfect. We're all perfect. It's just that things around us are so weird. I promise, I'll think. Goodbye. (*Hangs up*.) And I will. I'm crazy right? I AM A GODDAMN MENTAL CASE! I NEED TO BE PUT AWAY! SOMEBODY DROPPED ME ON MY HEAD WHEN I WAS A BABY! Here's this adorable man, after me! And how long have I yearned for this to happen, for somebody to sweep me off my feet and not take no for an answer? A million goddamned years I've yearned and pined.

And here it is, right on my doorstep. I dunno Jake, I'll just think about it, don't push me.

Cynthia is just an excuse! She won't care. It's me! I'm afraid! What if he doesn't love me anymore in a month, two months, a year, a decade? What if he leaves me all alone so that I dry up like a dead leaf? I WANT LOVE INSURANCE!

Well, fuck it, I'm changing, as of now. I'm not going to measure my life with coffee spoons. I'm going to dare to eat that peach. I am going to get all dressed up, (*SHE starts dressing.*) put on a silky garter belt, seamed stockings, a drop-dead dress, I am going to buy a bunch of roses, and I am going over that that man's apartment right now and throw my body on his. Damn the torpedoes, full speed ahead!

(*PHONE rings.*)

CLEO. Hello?

RITA. I'm so mad I could just spit.

CLEO. Gain some weight?

RITA. It's that fucking Kiwi. He's done it again.

CLEO. Oh, Jesus, the hibiscus tea drinker?

RITA. One and the same. She caught them walking down the street, hand in hand. Clothes on inside out.

CLEO. The motherfucker! Why? We know he loves her.

RITA. Some men just need constant drama, hon. He burst into tears and sobbed and went all crazy and asked her to marry him.

CLEO. What did she do?

RITA. She kicked him out. Killed her but she did it. Threw everything he owned out the window. She likes throwing things out windows. We'll have to stand by our girl, hon, she's going to have a rocky few months ahead of her. I just called Jake, he's on his way over there. Lucky nothing happened between you two. I don't think she could stand it now.

CLEO. Yes. Well, I'd better call. (*SHE dials phone.*)

CYNTHIA'S ANSWERING MACHINE. Thank you for calling the Larabee Cinema. Today's feature is "Girl Down the Tubes" a hilarious tale of betrayal, loss and anguish. Show time on the hour, every hour. Open all night. (*Beep.*)

CLEO. Ha ha, Cynthia. A laugh riot. Pick up your phone, please, talk, to me.

(*RITA dials phone.*)

CYNTHIA'S ANSWERING MACHINE. If this is who it always is, please get fucked. It's over. Pretend I'm dead. (*Beep*.)

RITA. Cynthia, it's Rita. You know, your friend? I know you're there.

(*CLEO dials phone*.)

CYNTHIA'S ANSWERING MACHINE. Please hang up. There appears to be a receiver off the hook. (*Beep*.)

CLEO. Cynthia? Are you there? It's been too long since we've heard from you. Are you okay? Cynthia? Please pick up. Okay, we're coming over.

Scene 13: ABYSS

CYNTHIA. (*Reading magazine*.) I don't know whether to kill myself or go bowling. Florence Henderson, on the love boat. (*Throws down the magazine*.)

RITA. Will you look at this shameless slut? Three in the afternoon and she's lying here in her second best nightgown.

CLEO. Pitiful.

RITA. Honey, when was the last time you washed your hair?

CYNTHIA. How the hell did you get in here? Go away, beat it, piss off.

CLEO. I used my key. You may have noticed that you have been completely incommunicado for weeks. You haven't even answered your phone. A sure attention getter.

RITA. Get up. Go take a shower.

CYNTHIA. What's the matter with me? I think I'm having a nervous breakdown. I just lie around all day, being sucked deeper and deeper into some crazy black whirlpool of the soul. Try and guess how many boxes of Oreo cookies I've gone through. How many Sara Lee brownies. Then, as a joke, I try to go out, take a little stroll in the hopes that it will make me feel somewhat normal. Immediately my heart starts jumping into my throat and I panic and think I'm having a heart attack.

CLEO. You are having a heart attack. Your heart's broken.

RITA. You've been flirting too long with the abyss. You've fallen in. It's time to pull yourself out. Scramble up those rocks. Get dirt under your fingernails. Hang tough. Wait it out. Jake's on his way over. He'll slap some sense into you.

CYNTHIA. With friends like you, who needs a mother? Anyway, I'm not heartbroken. I know it would never work. He was too young. He hadn't any sense of his own mortality.

RITA. Nobody who wasn't heartbroken would let her hair get into such a state. There is a palpable haze of self-pity enveloping you. I can hardly make you out. Take a shower, wash your hair.

CYNTHIA. I loved him though. For real. We had some kind of fearsome, intense connection. We would look at each other and be hypnotized. The smell of him lost me to the rest of the world. I was disgusting. I would sniff his armpits like a greedy puppy sniffs a crotch. I remember the very last time he sat on the edge of my bed, in an old pink T-shirt I bought for him—the line of his torso was incredibly dear to me.

CLEO. Not heartbroken. Not at all. No way.

RITA. Why not just pop into the shower and then tell us about it? I am not one of those people who gets her kicks from smelling pungent armpits.

CYNTHIA. (*Sniffing under her arm.*) Jesus, that proves it, I'm alive. Anyway, you don't understand. It's not about being heartbroken, I'm over that part. I'm sad, I'm resigned, I'm mending according to schedule. But this whole adventure has thrown me back on myself. And I can't stand the sight of my inner being. It's all bleak and horrible and useless and aching and needy and lonely and desperate. I have no inner resources, nothing will ever work.

RITA. I have turned the shower water on. Get in there before I cut that rancid nightgown off you.

CYNTHIA. Fascist! (*SHE goes into shower.*)

JAKE. Where is she?

CLEO. Shower.

RITA. Jake, get in there.

CYNTHIA. Jake, you pervert. Get out. I'm naked.

JAKE. I've seen them before, remember? Hi there, tits. Nice to see you again. Always loved them tits. I'll be right here until you're finished.

CYNTHIA. I'm not going to kill myself in the shower, you know.

JAKE. Course not.

CYNTHIA. I will be fine.

JAKE. Course you will. That boyfriend of yours has a new full time bimbo, I hear. You've probably heard too.

CYNTHIA. He's not my boyfriend anymore.

JAKE. And you're not sleeping with anyone. You have no distractions. The big old abandonment goblin has got you in its clutches. You're probably ready to spit.

CYNTHIA. This is not right, Jake. You were my boyfriend once. Why are we talking like this?

JAKE. This is where an old boyfriend can come in handy. I'm here to commiserate with you. Fold you in my large and masculine embrace. Soothe your troubled brow. Being abandoned by a loved one is the worst pain there is. It confirms our deepest fears.

CYNTHIA. We broke up. He has every right to go off with someone else.

JAKE. Course he does.

CYNTHIA. Jake, I want to kill him. I want to take an axe and split his head open. I want to kick him so hard in the balls that he's doubled up for a year. I want to have him arrested.

(During this exchange CLEO has come up to Jake and started absently rubbing him on the shoulder. SHE's whispering words of encouragement, patting, touching, HE likes it. As CYNTHIA comes out of the bathroom on "have him arrested" SHE sees them in a semi-embrace, forehead to forehead.)

RITA. *(Sidling up, adjusting Cynthia's towel with a tender, maternal gesture.)* Ain't love grand, darling.

CYNTHIA. I feel like I've been punched in the face. How long has this been going on?

RITA. Hasn't. Just started.

CYNTHIA. I could kill them both. Talk about timing. *(SHE disappears into "bathroom.")* YOU MOTHERFUCKERS! TRAITORS! I HATE YOUR FUCKING GUTS! *(Terrific crash, then CYNTHIA reappears with two glasses of water, which SHE proceeds to throw in Cleo and Jake's faces.)* Whew. There. I feel better now.

CLEO. Okay?

CYNTHIA. Yeah.

RITA. Darlin, you go put on your prettiest party dress and let's you and me go out and cut a rug. We dancing girls have just gotta keep on dancing, you know. Just keep on dancing.

Scene 14:   FEAR OF DATING

CYNTHIA. The realization hits me heavily, like a .44 magnum smashing into my skull. My heart starts beating with a quick dread and my blood freezes in my veins. My stomach does backflips. The ordeal I am about to face is one of the most chilling, grisly and macabre experiences know to woman.

Dating. I will have to start dating again.

Please God no, don't make me do it! I'll be good from now on, I promise! I'll stop feeding the dog hashish! I'll be kind, thoughtful, sober, industrious, anything. But please God, not the ultimate torture of dating!

That's why I stayed with him so long, probably. I couldn't stand going through it all again. Sure, he might be a trifle wild and intractable, I kept telling myself, but at least I know I'll get laid tonight, and tomorrow night. At least someone will go to the movies with me and try to hold my hand.

Hand-holding. The WORST thing about dating: The fellow, or maybe even I, will decide that holding hands is a sweet, simple way to start. Hah! It's the most nerve-wracking experience of life! Once I start holding hands, I'm afraid to stop. If I pull my hand away, will he think I'm being cold or moody? Should I squeeze his hand and kind of wiggle my fingers around suggestively? Or is that too forward? What if we're holding hands in the movies and I have to scratch my nose? If I let his hand go, then scratch the offending nose, and then not grab his hand again immediately will he think I'm rejecting him? Will he be relieved? What if my hand is clammy? A clammy hand is more offensive than bad breath or right-wing politics! A clammy hand means you are a lousy lay! Everybody knows that!

And what, dear spiteful God, will I wear? I'll need new dresses, new jewelry, new sweaters, trousers, underwear. And shoes! Shoes tell everything, shoes have to be perfect! Men like high heels, right? I can't walk in high heels. Well, I can try. For a really important date, I can just see myself spending $250 on a pair of drop dead heels. This time will be different, I'll tell myself, this time I will be able to walk. But after an hour the ball of my foot will cramp up, I know it, and I'll hobble. "Is anything wrong?" he'll ask me solicitously, "you're limping." And I won't be able to say these fucking shoes are crippling me and if I don't take them off this minute I'll be maimed for life! Because then he'll know I just bought them, that I bought them to go out on a date with him. And that will make him feel all weird and pressured to know that this date was a big deal for me and he'll realize that I'm not as popular and sophisticated as he thought I was if I had to buy a special pair of shoes that I can't even walk in for chrissakes just for a date with *him*. So I have to explain the limping in such a way that it won't have to do with shoes. And old war wound?

What if my hair refuses to behave? ~~What if it's all recalcitrant and cranky and goes all limp and flat on one side and then sort of bends at a right angle over one ear? I mean, sometimes I apply precisely the right amount of gel and hang upside down when I blow-dry it and yet something still goes drastically wrong and I end up looking like Margaret Thatcher.~~ Sometimes the suspense of what I will look like is so terrible that I have to take a Valium.

I have been known to apply four shades of lipstick, one on top of the other, in a pathetic attempt to achieve a certain I'm-not-actually-wearing-lipstick-I-just-naturally-have-pink-moist-luscious-lips effect. I have been known to put green eye-pencil below my lower lashes, look in the mirror, realize that I look like a gangrenous raccoon, quickly remove it, look in the mirror, realize that I'd rather look like a gangrenous raccoon than an anemic buffalo, and reapply the stuff. I have been known to start trying on outfits in an entirely tidy room and somehow when I am finished every single item of clothing I own is off the rack and on the floor and then when the phone rings there is no way on earth I can find it. I can't even find my *bed*. God, I hate dati·

And when he rings my doo ꜰell and my stockings are still around my ankles because my garter belt is missing but with mad, deep quick thought I finally remember it's in my black satin purse (don't ask) and I get it on and get the stockings up and answer the door smiling casually what precisely do I say?

WHAT WILL I TALK ABOUT ON A DATE?

Not one thing that's on my mind will be a suitable topic of conversation. "Do you think we'll sleep together tonight?" "Are you one of those guys who can't make a commitment? Or can only make a commitment to a woman with really smooth, finely muscled thighs?" "Is my deodorant working?" "What kind of relationship did you have with your mother?" "How do you think we're getting along so far?" "Do you like me?" "How much do you like me?" "Are you sure you really like me?" "Dated any junkies?" "You're not going out with me because you feel sorry for me, are you?"

No, we'll talk about movies. What we've seen recently. What if he tells me that he just got around to renting *Ford Fairlane*, and it wasn't so bad, really? Will I pretend to agree? I bet I will. I bet something slimy inside myself will cause me to nod my head encouragingly and say "Yes, wasn't it interesting?" And then I'll hate myself because I've turned our date into a tissue of lies. I'll become distracted thinking about what a hypocrite I really am and my eyes will glaze over and I'll nod absently when he tries to draw me out and then he'll get all paranoid, thinking I hate him because he liked *Ford Fairlane*. He'll be right.

But what if it turns out that his favorite movie is *His Girl Friday*, with *Slapshot* a close second?

Then I could fall in love. Then I'll really be terrified.

Scene 15: THRIFT SHOP

LURENE is sorting the clothes. An older man is behind a counter.

CLEO. (*Rushes in.*) Am I the first one? Has Cynthia been here yet? Is that the new stuff?

LURENE. We're not even open yet, hon. You're the first. I haven't even set up. Nice silk bed-jacket just came in, over there.

CLEO. I have enough bed jackets to outfit the Pittsburgh Steelers.

RITA. (*Entering.*) Cleo, I know a thrift store overexcites you, but did you have to push me in front of a bus just to get here first?

CLEO. All's fair in love and thrift shops.

RITA. (*Looking through a pile of things, not listening.*) Hmmm ...

CLEO. (*Pointing out window.*) Look, Robert Redford! Denzel Washington! (*As RITA looks CLEO pulls an item from the pile Rita was looking through and brings it over to the window.*) Oh well, guess I was mistaken.

RITA. Get a life! (*Points out window.*) Look! Jake! With a blonde! (*Grabs item back.*)

CLEO. (*Looking.*) Really? My darling? Oh my God. The Kiwi!

CYNTHIA. (*Entering*.) I'm too smart for her.

LURENE. He's cuter than ever, the slimeball. (*SHE exits*.)

CYNTHIA. (*Runs up*.) I see him. Oh, do I see him. Don't wave.

CLEO. Who would wave? He's wearing a fake leather jacket made out of some desperately ugly foam stuff.

RITA. You can call that at fifty feet?

CYNTHIA. Maybe he sees us. Maybe I should talk to him.

RITA. You need to get your perspective back first. That will take approximately another ten weeks.

CYNTHIA. More? I feel in my heart that I'm almost over that little shit.

RITA. Don't go near him. Addictions are relentless.

CYNTHIA. I love this place. A thrift shop is full of infinite pleasures and possibilities, mystical, healing, calm and joyous.

RITA. She does run on.

CLEO. I'm going to look at the ball gowns.

(*THEY exit*.)

MAN. You're my kind of woman.

(*CYNTHIA looks around, sees nothing*.)

MAN. It's the way you go through every box, looking behind and under things, ablaze with curiosity.

CYNTHIA. Look. Green suede gloves. Fifty cents.

MAN. Used to belong to Eulalia Henderson. Who was a devil with the men in her prime. Died last year at eighty-six.

CYNTHIA. Think they'll bring me luck?

MAN. I used to be a physicist. Knew everything. Gave it up. Over in that pile there you'll find a tea towel embroidered with spaceships and puppies. You'll like that.

CYNTHIA. (*Finds it.*) I guess you do know everything.

MAN. You also have a sad, lonely look in your eye. This worries me.

RITA. (*From back.*) Cynthia, are orange heels ever appropriate?

CYNTHIA. Not even in death. (*Back to man.*) Well, I am sad.

MAN. Here's something I know. I know that even the physicists have discovered chaos. That's what the big guys study now—the Chaos theory.

CYNTHIA. Meaning?

MAN. Meaning that nothing is predictable. Nothing in the universe is predictable. So there's no point in you having that fatal look in your eye.

CYNTHIA. I've lost my true love, my biological clock is running down, the world seems strange and ugly and I'm feeling tired and feeble and weird.

MAN. Ah, chicken shit. (*Takes photo from wallet.*) Here's my Sadie. Died last January. She's happy. I'm happier. I'm still alive. Who knows what's going to happen next? You look like you've got the capacity for about three more true loves and ten children who'll up and leave like they're supposed to. You have to have faith. Walk around those blind corners.

CYNTHIA. Are we entering into a religious discussion here?

MAN. Hell, I doubt it. I'm just shooting the breeze.

CYNTHIA. Here's all I know. There are certain tricks. One trick is not forgetting a thing. The way the sweat beads on a lover's brow when he's lying. The way a mother turns her back, the way a friend confesses her secrets.

CLEO. (*Offstage.*) Oh, Cynthia, come look, this is perfect for you!

MAN. Here's something I know. You never get anywhere until you figure out the difference between passion and compassion. Love affairs that begin in passion burn themselves out real quick, like blue stars. You gotta watch out for them, they can burn you up too. But then there's the love affairs that begin in compassion, those are the ones you want to find. They just build and build into real passion and then, well, then it's like you you can just drive into the sky, right up into and right past those blue stars.

CYNTHIA. So have faith?

MAN. Have faith in your own sinew, your nerve endings. Stop talking to an old man in a thrift shop and go out and kick some ass.

CYNTHIA. I'm already gone.

End of Play

CEMENTVILLE
by Jane Martin
Comedy
Little Theatre

(5m., 9f.) Int. The comic sensation of the 1991 Humana Festival at the famed Actors Theatre of Louisville, this wildly funny new play by the mysterious author of *Talking With* and *Vital Signs* is a brilliant portrayal of America's fascination with fantasy entertainment, "the growth industry of the 90's." We are in a run-down locker room in a seedy sports arena in the Armpit of the Universe, "Cementville, Tennessee," with the scurviest bunch of professional wrasslers you ever saw. This is decidedly a small-time operation—not the big time you see on TV. The promoter, Bigman, also appears in the show. He and his brother Eddie are the only men, though; for the main attraction(s) are the "ladies." There's Tiger, who comes with a big drinking problem and a small dog; Dani, who comes with a large chip on her shoulder against Bigman, who owes all the girls several weeks' pay; Lessa, an ex-Olympic shotputter with delusions that she is actually employed presently in athletics; and Netty, an overweight older woman who appears in the ring dressed in baggy pajamas, with her hair in curlers, as the character "Pajama Mama." There is the eager-beaver go-fer Nola, a teenager who dreams of someday entering the glamorous world of pro wrestling herself. And then, there are the Knockout Sisters, refugees from the Big Time but banned from it for heavy-duty abuse of pharmaceuticals as well as having gotten arrested *in flagrante delicto* with the Mayor of Los Angeles. They have just gotten out of the slammer; but their indefatigable manager, Mother Crocker ("Of the Auto-Repair Crockers") hopes to get them reinstated, if she can keep them off the white powder. Bigman has hired the Knockout Sisters as tonight's main attraction, and the fur really flies along with the sparks when the other women find out about the Knockout Sisters. Bigman has really got his hands full tonight. He's gotta get the girls to tear each other up in the ring, not the locker room; he's gotta deal with tough-as-nails Mother Crocker; he's gotta keep an arena full of tanked-up rubes from tearing up the joint—and he's gotta solve the mystery of who bit off his brother Eddie's dick last night.   (#5580)

I STAND BEFORE YOU NAKED
by Joyce Carol Oates
Monologues

(Little Theatre) 11f. (doubling possible—original production was done with 6f.) Bare stage. This extraordinary new collection of dramatic monologues by one of America's foremost novelists, poets, essayists and women of letters rivals *Talking With* in dramatic intensity, language and sheer weirdness. The evening begins and ends with the title poem, a haunting evocation of Woman on the edge of the madness of vulnerability. There is humor here, but mostly the monologues grip us in the firm hold of a master writer interested more in the pathetic, the strange, the horrifying. In other words, this is vintage Joyce Carol Oates. Contains the following monologues: "Little Blood Button," "Wife of," "Wealthy Lady," "The Boy," "The Orange," "Good Morning, Good Afternoon," "Darling, I'm Telling You (Angel Eyes)," "Nuclear Holocaust," "Slow Motion," "Pregnant."   (#11681)

VITAL SIGNS
by Jane Martin
Monologue play

(Little Theatre) 2m., (optional), 6f. Bare stage. The mysterious, pseudonymous Louisvillian, author of the acclaimed *Talking With,* has never been funnier, or more dramatically compelling, than in this extraordinary suite of theatrical miniatures, over thirty monologues with a length of around two minutes each, for six actresses. The two men in the play are "foils" for these compelling women. Although they do speak in one piece, their presence in your cast may be optional. Somehow, all the pieces add up to a collage of contemporary woman in all her warmth and majesty, her fear and frustration, her joy and her sadness. *Vital Signs* wowed them at the Humana Festival at Actors Theatre of Louisville, where its exciting first production was staged by Artistic Director Jon Jory. Included in our book are the details of Mr. Jory's direction which kept the theatrical ball rolling, headed into the pocket for a strike. "It does not just celebrate language from colorful women; [it] does the hoe-down."—Detroit Free Press. The New York Times praised "the continuing vitality and originality of the author's voice." "Offers wonderful opportunities for actresses to show off their versatility."—Washington Times. "Martin's eye and ear for the texture of everyday life in this culture is as playfully accurate as Lily Tomlin and Jane Wagner's. She's a fine quipster; but she manages, too, to open little windows of sadness into women's souls."—Detroit News.   (#24019)

TWO NEW COMEDIES FROM
▬▬▬ SAMUEL FRENCH, Inc.▬▬▬

FAST GIRLS. (Little Theatre). Comedy. Diana Amsterdam. 2m., 3f. Int. Lucy Lewis is a contemporary, single woman in her thirties with what used to be called a "healthy sex life," much to the chagrin of her mother, who feels Lucy is too fast, too easy—and too single. Her best friend, on the other hand, neighbor Abigail McBride, is deeply envious of Lucy's ease with men. When Lucy wants to date a man she just calls him up, whereas Abigail sits home alone waiting for Ernest, who may not even know she exists, to call. The only time Abigail isn't by the phone is after Lucy has had a hot date, when she comes over to Lucy's apartment to hear the juicy details and get green with envy. Sometimes, though, Lucy doesn't want to talk about it, which drives Abigail *nuts* ("If you don't tell me about men I have no love life!"). Lucy's mother arrives to take the bull by the horns, so to speak, arriving with a challenge. Mom claims no man will marry Lucy (even were she to *want to* get married), because she's too easy. Lucy takes up the challenge, announcing that she is going to get stalwart ex-boyfriend Sidney ("we're just friends") Epstein to propose to her. Easier said than done. Sidney doesn't *want* a fast girl. Maybe dear old Mom is right, thinks Lucy. Maybe fast girls *can't* have it all. "Amsterdam makes us laugh, listen and think."—Daily Record. "Brilliantly comic moments."—The Monitor. "rapidly paced comedy with a load of laughs . . . a funny entertainment with some pause for reflection on today's [sexual] confusion."—Suburban News. "Takes a penetrating look at [contemporary sexual chaos]. Passion, celibacy, marriage, fidelity are just some of the subjects that Diana Amsterdam hilariously examines."—Tribune News. (#8149)

ADVICE FROM A CATERPILLAR. (Little Theatre.) Comedy. Douglas Carter Beane. 2m. 2f. 1 Unit set & 1 Int. Ally Sheedy and Dennis Christopher starred in the delightful off-Broadway production of this hip new comedy. Ms. Sheedy played Missy, an avant garde video artist who specializes in re-runs of her family's home videos, adding her own disparaging remarks. Needless to say, she is very alienated from the middle-class, family values she grew up with, which makes her very *au courant*, but strangely unhappy. She has a successful career and a satisfactory love-life with a businessman named Suit. Suit's married, but that doesn't stop him and Missy from carrying on. Something's missing, though—and Missy isn't sure what it is, until she meets Brat. He is a handsome young aspiring actor. Unfortunately, Brat is also the boyfriend of Missy's best friend. Sound familiar? It isn't—because Missy's best friend is a gay man named Spaz! Spaz has been urging Missy to find an unmarried boyfriend, but this is too much—too much for Spaz, too much for Suit and, possibly, too much for Missy. Does she *want* a serious relationship (ugh—how bourgeois!)? Can a bisexual unemployed actor actually be her Mr. Wonderful? "Very funny ... a delightful evening."—Town & Village. (#3876)

✔✔✔✔✔✔✔✔✔✔✔✔✔✔✔✔✔✔✔✔✔✔✔✔✔✔✔

OTHER PUBLICATIONS FOR YOUR INTEREST

COASTAL DISTURBANCES
(Little Theatre- Comedy)

by TINA HOWE

3 male, 4 female

This new Broadway hit from the author of *PAINTING CHURCHES,
MUSEUM,* and *THE ART OF DINING* is quite daring and experimental,
in that it is *not* cynical or alienated about love and romance. This is an
ensemble play about four generations of vacationers on a
Massachusetts beach which focuses on a budding romance between a
hunk of a lifeguard and a kooky young photographer. Structured as a
series of vignettes taking place over the course of the summer, the
play looks at love from all sides now. "A modern play about love that
is, for once, actually about love--as opposed to sexual, social or
marital politics . . . it generously illuminates the intimate landscape
between men and women." --NY Times. "Enchanting."--New Yorker.
#5755

APPROACHING ZANZIBAR
(Advanced Groups—Comedy)

by TINA HOWE

2 male, 4 female, 3 children --Various Ints. and Exts.

This new play by the author of *Painting Churches, Coastal
Disturbances, Museum,* and *The Art of Dining* is about the cross-
country journey of the Blossom family--Wallace and Charlotte and
their two kids Turner and Pony--out west to visit Charlotte's aunt
Olivia Childs in Taos, New Mexico. Aunt Olivia, a renowned
environmental artist who creates enormous "sculptures" of hundreds of
kites, is dying of cancer, and Charlotte wants to see her one last time.
The family camps out along the way, having various adventures and
meeting other relatives and strangers, until, eventually, they arrive in
Taos, where Olivia is fading in and out of reality--or is she? Little
Pony Blossom persuades the old lady to stand up and jump up and down
on the bed, and we are left with final entrancing image of Aunt Olivia
and Pony bouncing on the bed like a trampoline. Has a miracle
occurred? "What pervades the shadow is Miss Howe's originality and
purity of her dramatic imagination."--The New Yorker. #3140

Other Publications for Your Interest

TALKING WITH . . .
(LITTLE THEATRE)
By JANE MARTIN

11 women—Bare stage

Here, at last, is the collection of eleven extraordinary monologues for eleven actresses which had them on their feet cheering at the famed Actors Theatre of Louisville—audiences, critics and, yes, even jaded theatre professionals. The mysteriously pseudonymous Jane Martin is truly a ''find'', a new writer with a wonderfully idiosyncratic style, whose characters alternately amuse, move and frighten us always, however, speaking to use from the depths of their souls. The characters include a baton twirler who has found God through twirling; a fundamentalist snake handler, an ex-rodeo rider crowded out of the life she has cherished by men in 3-piece suits who want her to dress up ''like Minnie damn Mouse in a tutu''; an actress willing to go to any length to get a job; and an old woman who claims she once saw a man with ''cerebral walrus'' walk into a McDonald's and be healed by a Big Mac. ''Eleven female monologues, of which half a dozen verge on brilliance.''—London Guardian. ''Whoever (Jane Martin) is, she's a writer with an original imagination.''—Village Voice. ''With Jane Martin, the monologue has taken on a new poetic form, intensive in its method and revelatory in its impact.''—Philadelphia Inquirer. ''A dramatist with an original voice . . . (these are) tales about enthusiasms that become obsessions, eccentric confessionals that levitate with religious symbolism and gladsome humor.''—N.Y. Times. *Talking With . . .* is the 1982 winner of the American Theatre Critics Association Award for Best Regional Play. (#22009)

HAROLD AND MAUDE
(ADVANCED GROUPS—COMEDY)
By COLIN HIGGINS

9 men, 8 women—Various settings

Yes: *the Harold and Maude!* This is a stage adaptation of the wonderful movie about the suicidal 19 year-old boy who finally learns how to truly *live* when he meets up with that delightfully whacky octogenarian, Maude. Harold is the proverbial Poor Little Rich Kid. His alienation has caused him to attempt suicide several times, though these attempts are more cries for attention than actual attempts. His peculiar attachment to Maude, whom he meets at a funeral (a mutual passion), is what saves him—and what captivates us. This new stage version, a hit in France directed by the internationally-renowned Jean-Louis Barrault, will certainly delight both afficionados of the film and new-comers to the story. ''Offbeat upbeat comedy.''—Christian Science Monitor. (#10032)

NEW COMEDIES FROM
SAMUEL FRENCH, INC.

MAIDS OF HONOR. (Little Theatre.) Comedy. Joan Casademont. 3m., 4f. Comb Int./Ext. Elizabeth McGovern, Laila Robins and Kyra Sedgwick starred in this warm, wacky comedy at Off-Broadway's famed WPA Theatre. Monica Bowlin, a local TV talk-show host, is getting married. Her two sisters, Isabelle and Annie, are intent on talking her out of it. It seems that Mr. Wonderful, the groom-to-be, is about to be indicted for insider trading, a little secret he has failed to share with his fiancee, Monica. She has a secret she has kept herself, too—she's pregnant, possibly not by her groom-to-be! All this is uncovered by delightfully kookie Isabelle, who aspires to be an investigative reporter. She'd also like to get Monica to realize that she is marrying the wrong man, for the wrong reason. She should be marrying ex-boyfriend Roger Dowling, who has come back to return a diary Monica left behind. And sister Annie should be marrying the caterer for the wedding, old flame Harry Hobson—but for some reason she can't relax enough to see how perfect he is for her. The reason for all three Bowlin women's difficulties with men, the reason why they have always made the wrong choice and failed to see the right one, is that they are the adult children of an alcoholic father and an abused mother, both now passed away, and they cannot allow themselves to love because they themselves feel unlovable. Sound gloomy and depressing? No, indeed. This delightful, wise and warm-hearted new play is loaded with laughs. We would also like to point out to all you actors that the play is also loaded with excellent monologues, at least one of which was recently included in an anthology of monologues from the best new plays.)   (#14961)

GROTESQUE LOVESONGS. (Little Theatre.) Comedy. Don Nigro. (Author of *The Curate Shakespeare As You Like It, Seascape with Sharks and Dancer* and other plays). This quirky new comedy about a family in Terre Haute, Indiana, enchanted audiences at NYC's famed WPA Theatre. Two brothers, Pete and John, live with their parents in a big old house with an attached greenhouse. The father, Dan, has a horticulture business. A pretty young woman named Romy is more or less engaged to marry younger brother Johnny as the play begins, and their prospects look quite rosy, for Johnny has just inherited a ton of money from recently-deceased family friend, Mr. Agajanian. Why, wonders Pete, has Agajanian left his entire estate to Johnny? He starts to persistently ask this question to his mother, Louise. Eventually, Louise does admit that, in fact, Mr. Agajanian was Johnny's father. This news stuns Johnny; but he's not *really* staggered until he goes down to the greenhouse and finds Pete and Romy making love. Pete, it seems, has always desperately wanted Romy; but when she chose Johnny instead he married a woman in the circus who turned out to be a con artist, taking him for everything he had and then disappearing. It seems everyone but Johnny is haunted by a traumatic past experience: Louise by her affair with Agajanian; Dan by the memory of his first true love, a Terre Haute whore; Pete by his failed marriage, and Romy by her *two* failed marriages. (One husband she left; the other was run over by a truckload of chickens [He loved cartoons so much, says Romy, that it was only fitting he should die like Wile E. Coyote.]). And, each character but Johnny knows what he wants. Louise and Dan want the contentment of their marriage; Romy wants to bake bread in a big old house—and she wants Pete, who finally admits that he wants her, too. And, finally, Johnny realizes what he wants. He does not want the money, or Agajanian's house. He wants to go to Nashville to make his own way as a singer of sad—yes, grotesque—love songs in the night. NOTE: this play is a treasure-trove of scene and monologue material.)   (#9925)